Barbie BIG CITY, BIG DREAMS™

Adapted by Marilyn Easton

Based on the script adaption by Lainee Gant and story
by Christopher Keenan & Kate Splaine

Art by Fernando Güell, Ferran Rodríguez & David Güell

studio fun
INTERNATIONAL

One summer morning, Barbie sat in the back of a taxi, looking out of the window at the bustling streets of New York City. Soon, she arrived at the Handler Arts Academy, where she was going to spend the summer perfecting her performing arts talents.

But first, she needed to find her room.

Barbie felt a rush of excitement when she finally spotted her name on one of the doors. But she also felt confused—another girl was standing in front of the same door.

"I'm Barbie Roberts," they said in unison.

The girls were shocked! They shared the same name! Barbie from Malibu, California, discovered her new roommate was Barbie from Brooklyn, New York.

They decided to call each other "Malibu" and "Brooklyn."

Brooklyn offered to show Malibu around the city. They strolled through Central Park, snapped a picture in front of a Broadway theater, and even ate hot dogs from a street cart vendor.

On the subway ride back, Malibu spotted an ad featuring her favorite pop star, Emmie.

"I have all her albums!" Malibu squealed.

Brooklyn sadly looked away.

"Wait, you're not a fan?" Malibu asked.

"We used to be best friends until she became famous," Brooklyn explained, trying to hide the hurt in her voice.

The next day, all of the summer program students sat in the theater, buzzing with excitement. Dean Morrison announced that she and the instructors would observe their classes to select one winner for the Spotlight Solo. It was going to stream live from Times Square!

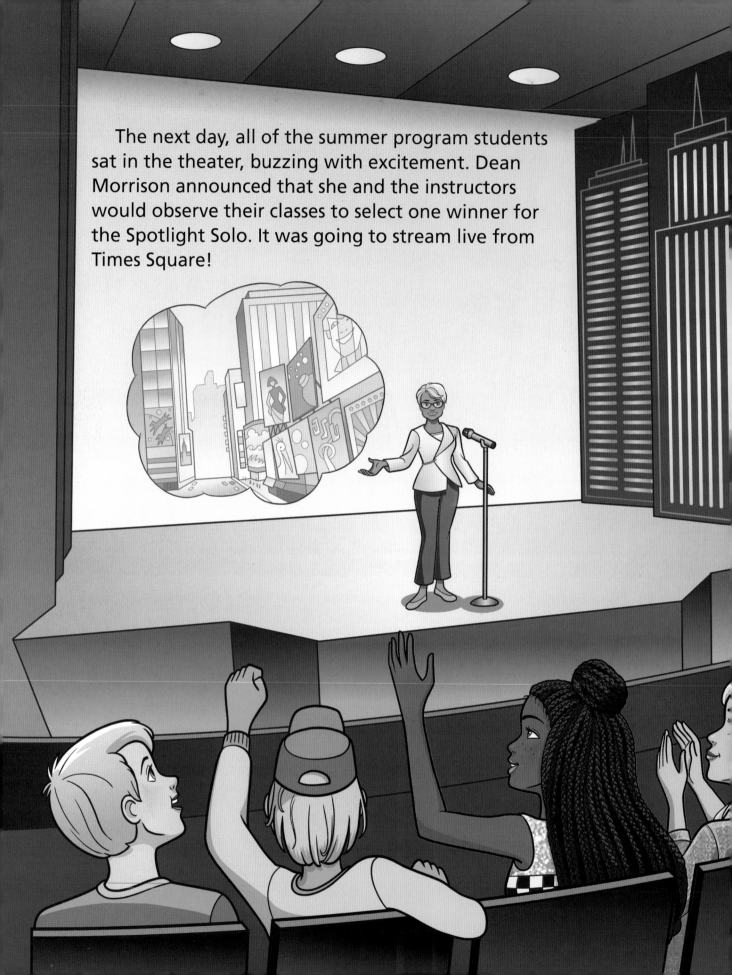

Later in dance class, Malibu missed a dance step right in front of Dean Morrison! She hoped it didn't ruin her chances of winning the Spotlight Solo.

But her stumbling didn't stop there.

In stage combat class, her sword flew out of her hand.

In music class, her guitar was completely off-key.

Brooklyn gave Malibu a comforting smile. At least they were in this together.

In the cafeteria, Brooklyn and Malibu sat with their new friend, Rafa, and a girl they hadn't met before named Lee.

Suddenly, Brooklyn realized she had met Lee before. Only her name wasn't Lee. She was her friend Emily, who became the famous pop star Emmie! But why was she wearing glasses and a wig?

Lee explained she was wearing a disguise because she wanted to be taken seriously at the program. She didn't want to be treated differently just because she was Emmie.

Everyone agreed to keep Lee's secret.

Lee apologized to Brooklyn for losing touch. "When my dad became my manager, I just stopped having a life," she explained.

Later that day, Brooklyn and Malibu were going over some choreography from class. Malibu was still having trouble with the moves and was thankful for her friend's help.

Brooklyn was feeling thankful as well, but for a different reason.

"I'm so happy Emily—I mean Lee—is back in my life," Brooklyn said. "And relieved it was her dad who dumped me and not her. Thank goodness my mom's a pilot and not my manager!"

When they got back to the academy, Dean Morrison was introducing Mr. Miller from the board of directors. He was going to observe their classes.

Lee was shocked and upset. Mr. Miller was her father!

Afterward, she confronted him.

Lee's dad explained he was there to ensure she won the Spotlight Solo. If Lee didn't win, it would damage her career.

"I'm not here to win," she insisted. "I'm here to learn."

But her father refused to listen.

Lee joined her friends onstage while they waited for their dance instructor to arrive. The girls started warming up and dancing around. Rafa was there too, recording the action on his phone. Malibu started spinning while her friends cheered her on. But then Malibu completely lost her balance. She tried to steady herself, but she accidentally knocked Brooklyn off the stage!

Malibu was very worried about her friend. She was relieved when they found out Brooklyn just had a sprained ankle. She would be better in a few days.

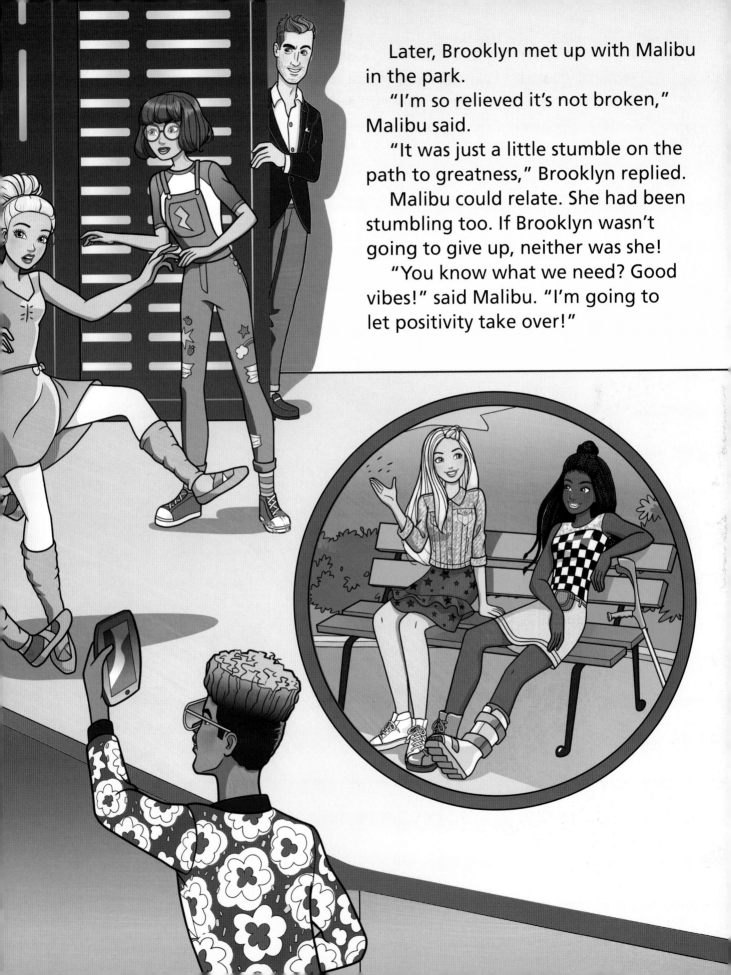

Later, Brooklyn met up with Malibu in the park.

"I'm so relieved it's not broken," Malibu said.

"It was just a little stumble on the path to greatness," Brooklyn replied.

Malibu could relate. She had been stumbling too. If Brooklyn wasn't going to give up, neither was she!

"You know what we need? Good vibes!" said Malibu. "I'm going to let positivity take over!"

Malibu began approaching her classes with confidence. She wasn't perfect, but she was doing her best and having fun. For the first time in a while, Malibu felt sure of herself.

But later, Dean Morrison called Malibu into her office.

The dean told her she was being cut from the program for intentionally pushing Brooklyn off the stage to get ahead of the competition!

"But it was an accident!" Malibu protested.

"You must leave the academy immediately," said the dean.

Malibu was heartbroken.

The dean then broke the news to Brooklyn. At first, Brooklyn defended Malibu, but then the dean revealed there was a witness.

"I thought we were friends," said Brooklyn as tears filled her eyes.

Malibu found Brooklyn in the music studio.
"You won't believe—" Malibu began.
"I already know. You pushed me to cut out the competition," Brooklyn said with disgust.
"What? No! It was an accident!" Malibu said.
She tried to defend herself, but Brooklyn wouldn't listen.
Malibu left. There was nothing else to say.

On her way to the airport, Malibu couldn't shake the feeling that something was missing. Then she realized she had left behind two important things—her friends and her dreams.

Meanwhile, Rafa and Lee refused to believe Malibu would deliberately hurt Brooklyn.

"That girl was all about friendship. She even made me promise not to post the video of you so your secret wouldn't leak," Rafa told Lee.

That's when they both realized Rafa had recorded the whole thing! The footage proved it was an accident and that the witness was Lee's father!

After reviewing the footage, Brooklyn and Dean Morrison regretted their mistake.

Luckily, Brooklyn knew exactly how to fix it.

Malibu was unpacking when she heard singing outside. It was Brooklyn!

"What are you doing here?" Malibu called out.

"I came to apologize," Brooklyn replied.

Malibu couldn't believe Brooklyn had flown across the country just to say sorry!

"Remember I told you my mom was a pilot?" Brooklyn laughed as her mom waved from the street. "Come on, you've been re-enrolled. I'll explain on the plane!"

Several nights later, a large crowd was gathered in the theater.

"Welcome to Handler Arts Academy's Spotlight Solo!" Dean Morrison announced. "And now, it's my pleasure to introduce . . . Barbie Roberts!"

Malibu and Brooklyn's heartfelt song was a promise to always be each other's fiercest competition, and to never let jealousy stand in their way.

Suddenly, another singer joined them onstage. It was Emmie!

In Times Square, an enormous screen lit up for everyone to see. On it were the smiling faces of not one . . . but two . . . Barbie Roberts!